E Kay

Kay, Verla.

Homespun Sarah /

PALM BEACH COUNTY
LIBRARY SYSTEM
3650 SUMMIT BLVD.
WEST PALM BEACH, FLORIDA 33406

Homespun Sarah

VERLA KAY

illustrated by

TED RAND

G. P. PUTNAM'S SONS • NEW YORK

To my wonderful aunt Verla
for being the very special person she is. —V. K.

To my daughter Theresa. —T. R.

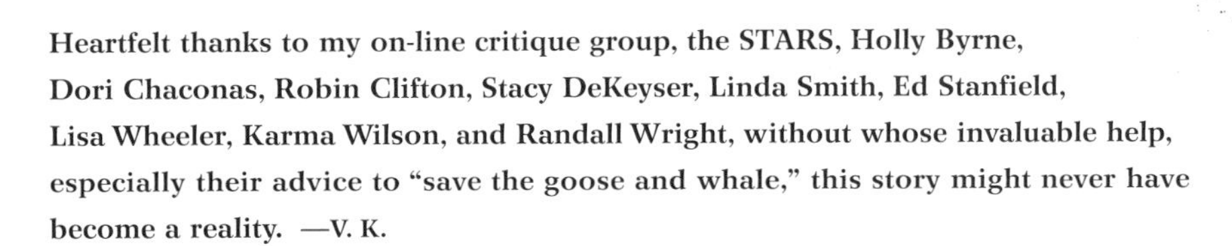

Heartfelt thanks to my on-line critique group, the STARS, Holly Byrne, Dori Chaconas, Robin Clifton, Stacy DeKeyser, Linda Smith, Ed Stanfield, Lisa Wheeler, Karma Wilson, and Randall Wright, without whose invaluable help, especially their advice to "save the goose and whale," this story might never have become a reality. —V. K.

Thanks to Pam Stitely and Sharon Burnston of the Colonial Pennsylvania Plantation for their careful examination of the sketches. —T. R.

Text copyright © 2003 by Verla Kay. Illustrations copyright © 2003 by Ted Rand. All rights reserved.
This book, or parts thereof, may not be reproduced in any form without permission in writing from the publisher,
G. P. Putnam's Sons, a division of Penguin Putnam Books for Young Readers, 345 Hudson Street, New York, NY 10014.
G. P. Putnam's Sons, Reg. U.S. Pat. & Tm. Off. Published simultaneously in Canada. Manufactured in China by South China Printing Co. (1988) Ltd. Designed by Gunta Alexander. Text set in Wilke Bold.
The art was done in traditional transparent watercolors, with acrylic medium, on ragstock paper.

Library of Congress Cataloging-in-Publication Data
Kay, Verla. Homespun Sarah / Verla Kay; illustrated by Ted Rand. p. cm. Summary: Simple rhyming text presents the everyday life of a young girl, living on a Pennsylvania farm in the early eighteenth century, who is quickly outgrowing her dress. [1. Farm life—Pennsylvania—Fiction. 2. Clothing and dress—Fiction. 3. Pennsylvania—Fiction. 4. Stories in rhyme.] I. Rand, Ted, ill. II. Title. PZ8.3.K225 Ho 2003 [E]—dc21 00-069678 ISBN 0-399-23417-9
10 9 8 7 6 5 4 3 2 1 First Impression

Author's Note

My fictional character Sarah lived in Pennsylvania in the early 1700s, when families living on farms had to raise, grow, and make almost everything they needed to survive. Most colonial homes were a single room, often with a sleeping loft for older children. Parents and younger children slept on the ground floor in front of the fireplace, and almost everyone slept on mats of rush or feathers, which were rolled up during the day.

Chairs were expensive and were usually used only by the father of the family—everyone else sat on benches or stools. But during meals, children were not allowed to sit, and they were NEVER allowed to speak while eating—for any reason at all.

The women of the house did the cooking, and in those days, many young women died from their clothing catching on fire. Spoons and knives were the only eating utensils, and often just one mug was passed around from person to person. Water was considered unsafe to drink, so everyone drank beer, including babies and children. (It was brewed to be barely alcoholic.)

New clothing was almost all handmade, and it was a very time-consuming process. A girl would wear her only dress every day for as long as it fit, *even if it was a year or more*. It was an exciting day when a girl got a new outfit to wear!

Homespun Sarah,
Braided head.
Warm quilt, snuggle,
Feather bed.

Rooster crowing,
Water, pour.
Bare toes prancing,
Chilly floor.

Sarah dressing,
Bodice, snug.
Ankles showing,
Long skirt, tug.

Winding pathway,
Singing lark.
Outhouse, smelly,
Creaky, dark.

Cold stream, bucket,
Water, spill.
Gather branches,
Wood box, fill.

Sarah's brother,
"Stand still, cow!"
Father dusty,
Mule and plow.

Planting furrows,
Shearing sheep.
Sarah weeding,
Chickens peep.

One-room cabin,
Fireplace, hooks.
Big pot steaming,
Cornmeal cooks.

Hot flames, sparking,
Mother jumps.
Skirt hem burning!
Wet hand thumps.

Mugs of leather,
Home-brewed ale.
Soup of pumpkins,
Roasted quail.

Children standing,
Silent, still.
Spoons with tin plates,
Eating fill.

Sarah squirming,
Clothes too tight.
Laces straining,
Woeful sight.

Dirty laundry,
Giant tubs.
Lye soap, water,
Mother scrubs.

Bramble bushes,
Sarah, clothes.
Tending baby,
Wiping nose.

Beeswax, tallow,
Candlewicks.
Dipping, dripping,
Strings on sticks.

Flax plants ripen,
Flowers, blue.
Cornstalks waving,
"Blackbirds, SHOO!"

Picking berries,
"Ouch! A thorn!"
Wooden buckets,
Clothing, torn.

Bushes rustle,
Big black bear.
Sarah hiding,
Frightful scare!

Washing, drying,
Flax on racks.
Carding, combing,
Wool in sacks.

Sarah turning,
Spinning wheel.
Fingers busy,
Winding reel.

Dyeing, weaving,
Balls of thread.
Linsey-woolsey,
Blue and red.

Mother frowning,
Sarah, tall.
Bodice binding,
Dress, too small.

Homespun fabric,
Measure, clip.
Needles sewing,
Scissors snip.

Hand-stitched bodice,
Pulled and laced.
Long skirt flowing,
Just-right waist.

Spinning, twirling,
Dancing toes.
Homespun Sarah,
All new clothes!